Personal Space

VIOLET MACKEREL'S

Personal Space

Anna Branford

illustrated by Elanna Allen

Atheneum Books for Young Readers
New York   London   Toronto   Sydney   New Delhi

Atheneum Books For Young Readers

An imprint of Simon & Schuster Children's Publishing Division
1230 Avenue of the Americas, New York, New York 10020

For information about special discounts for bulk purchases, please contact
Simon & Schuster Special Sales at 1-866-506-1949
or business@simonandschuster.com.
The Simon & Schuster Speakers Bureau can bring authors to your live event.
For more information or to book an event,
contact the Simon & Schuster Speakers Bureau at 1-866-248-3049
or visit our website at www.simonspeakers.com.
Also available in an Atheneum Books for Young Readers hardcover edition.
Book design by Lauren Rille
The text for this book is set in Excelsior.
The illustrations for this book are rendered in pencil with digital ink.
Manufactured in the United States of America
1021 MTN

10 9 8 7
Library of Congress Cataloging-in-Publication Data
Branford, Anna.
Violet Mackerel's personal space / Anna Branford ; illustrated by
Elanna Allen.
p. cm.
Summary: Violet finds a special way to cope with moving to a new home
after Mama marries Vincent.
ISBN 978-1-4424-3591-9 (hardcover)
ISBN 978-1-4424-3592-6 (paperback)
ISBN 978-1-4424-3593-3 (eBook)
[1. Remarriage—Fiction. 2. Weddings—Fiction. 3. Moving, Household—Fiction.
4. Family life—Fiction.] I. Allen, Elanna, illustrator. II. Title.
PZ7.B737384Vhm 2013
[Fic]—dc23   2012025783

For Kate
(my sister)
—A. B.

For the remarkable J. K. R.
—E. A.

Personal Space

1 The Pink Shell

Violet Mackerel is on a summer holiday at the beach with her sister, Nicola; her brother, Dylan; her mama; and her mama's boyfriend, Vincent. It is nearly the end of the holiday, and Violet is wishing it was still the beginning.

At the beach house where they have been staying there are bunk beds. Violet has been sleeping on the bottom bunk. She has tucked a sheet under the mattress of the top bunk and dangled it down, so it is a small personal space of her own. You can't do that with an ordinary bed like the one at Violet's normal house. It has to be a bunk bed.

It has been quite a good holiday. Violet likes Vincent making pancakes for everyone each morning. She likes going for walks to look in rock pools and having the sound of the sea in her ears all the time. She likes it after dinner when they roll up their pants for an evening paddle and their pants get wet anyway and no one minds. And since no one has to get up at any particular time, no one has to go to bed at any particular time either, so they sit up late on the veranda, chatting and burning citronella candles to keep the mosquitoes away.

On the last morning of the holiday, everyone puts all their things back in their suitcases. Violet takes the sheet down from the bunk bed and folds it up. One minute it looks as if her family actually does live in the beach house, and the next minute it looks as if they have never stayed there at all.

Mama says, "Before we go, let's all have one final check and make sure we haven't left anything behind." So everyone has a look behind the couch and in the little cupboard in the bathroom and under the coffee table. Violet thinks

she might pull up the corner of her
mattress and have a look under that.
There is a row of flat wooden slats
with little spaces between them. And
in one of the spaces there is a small
pink shell.

It isn't one of Violet's shells. She has collected lots of shells, but they are packed carefully in a box in her suitcase with the pieces of sea glass she found on the beach. This pink shell has been left there by someone else.

Violet wonders who it could have been. Maybe it was someone else who slept on the bottom bunk and didn't want to go home. Maybe they left the small pink shell behind on purpose.

This thought gives Violet a good idea for a new theory, the Theory of Leaving Small Things Behind. The theory is this: Maybe wherever you leave something small behind, a tiny part of you gets to stay too.

Violet opens her suitcase, finds her box, and takes out a little piece of green sea glass. She presses it into

the space beside the pink shell and covers it all up again, smoothing the mattress. No one sees.

"Finished," calls Violet, going to join the others. She puts her suitcase next to Mama's in the trunk of the car.

Before they leave, she has one last look at the room. It looks exactly the same as it did before she stayed there. But it is not. Somehow this idea makes Violet feel a bit less sad about the summer holiday being finished.

It is a long drive from the beach back to her house, so she has lots of time to think about her new theory and about all the places she might like to leave small things. She would like to hide a sequin up the Eiffel Tower and bury a little glass bead somewhere in the African wilderness and slip a silver star under a stone in an Egyptian pyramid.

It will be like a little trail of Violet all throughout the world.

2 The Picnic Dinner

At home that evening, dinner is a funny mix of things that were in the kitchen before the holiday and are still okay to eat, like baked beans and corn chips and dried pawpaw spears, which Violet quite likes. But even though it is more like a picnic than actual dinner, Mama has put proper wineglasses on the table for everyone, and Vincent is filling them up with pink lemonade.

When everyone is sitting down, Vincent puts his arm around Mama and says, "We have some special news."

Violet nibbles a pawpaw spear and hopes that the news will be about getting a kitten.

"Vincent and I have decided we would like to get married," says Mama.

A funny feeling comes into the kitchen, and no one says anything.

Violet wants to say something, but it is hard to think of what. Last year her teacher, Miss Wuthering, got married and came back from her holiday being called Mrs. Chan.

She showed Violet's class a picture of herself in a long, white dress with sparkles in her hair.

"Will you change your name and put sparkles in your hair?" asks Violet.

"Well," says Mama, "I'll still be a Mackerel, but I might put sparkles in my hair."

Vincent says, "We were thinking we might have a small wedding in the garden and just invite a few special guests."

"Can I make paper cranes for the guests?" asks Nicola.

"We'd love that," says Vincent.

"Can I help you make a wedding dress?" asks Violet.

"Of course you can," says Mama.

Violet smiles, and Nicola is starting to smile too. Violet thinks Mama will look lovely with sparkles in her hair.

"But there isn't room in our house for any more people," says Dylan, who is not smiling. "We already hardly fit."

It is true that it's already sometimes a bit of a squish with Mama, Nicola, Dylan, and Violet, especially when they all need to go to the bathroom at exactly the same time.

"Well, that's the other part of the news," says Mama. "We'll have to move to a slightly bigger place if we're all going to live together. We're going to need to find a new home very soon, in fact."

"I'm not moving anywhere," says Dylan.

Then he goes upstairs and slams his bedroom door shut.

After that, the picnic dinner doesn't seem quite so nice.

3 The Shuffling Noise

Violet would like to knock on Dylan's door and see if he wants some pink lemonade or corn chips (she has eaten all the pawpaw spears), but Mama says Dylan's room is his personal space, and when he's inside it with the door closed, that means he probably just wants to be by himself for a while. So after dinner Violet goes up to her room and writes a small note with a pencil. It says:

Dear Dylan,

If you want more pink
lemonade and corn chips,
I could bring some
up to your room.
Knock three times
if you want me to.
Love from
Violet

At the end of the note she draws
a small violin, because Dylan is a
very good violin player, and a small
violet, because that is her name.
She slides the note under Dylan's
door and waits to see if there is any
knocking, but there is none—just a

strange shuffling and rummaging of things being moved around.

Later on, after Vincent has gone home, Mama chats with Nicola in her bedroom. Violet is still waiting outside Dylan's door in case there is any knocking. But there is only more shuffling and rummaging, and soon Mama comes out of Nicola's room and says it is time for bed. She tucks Violet in.

"Is Nicola okay?" asks Violet.

"I think so," says Mama.

"Is Dylan okay?" asks Violet.

"Not just at the moment," says Mama. "It will probably take us all a while to figure everything out."

Violet is mostly quite good at figuring things out. Even though she doesn't remember Dad very well, because he left when she was quite small, Violet knows that Dylan and Nicola both miss him, Dylan especially. Having a new person in your family is quite a big change to manage, especially if you are still missing an old one.

"What about you?" Mama asks. "Are you okay?"

Violet wonders whether or not she is okay.

"Well, I am glad there is going to be a wedding with sparkles in your hair and paper cranes for the guests," says Violet. "And I think it will be nice if Vincent lives with us and makes us pancakes every day."

Mama smiles.

"But I like us living here, even

if it is a squish," says Violet. "And I don't like people being not okay by themselves in their rooms, even if it is their personal space."

"Neither do I," says Mama.

Then they have quite a long cuddle, because it is very tricky getting to sleep when there are people in your house who are not okay. While she tries to sleep, Violet thinks about the tiny pink shell and the little piece of green sea glass hidden under the mattress at the beach house. If she closes her eyes, it's almost as if she is there again, with the sheet dangling down and the soft noise of the sea in her ears. It is a nice thought. Much nicer than the thought of a newer, bigger house, and much nicer than the thought of Dylan not being okay. The Theory of Leaving Small Things Behind is quite a good theory, she thinks.

4 The Leaky Tent

Very early the next morning the shuffling noise in Dylan's room goes all the way downstairs and out into the back garden. Sleepily Violet goes over to her window and looks outside. Dylan is putting up a tent that used to belong to Dad. Even though it is a bit leaky and musty, he keeps it in the back of his wardrobe, and he even took it on his school camping

trip last year. He said it was the worst tent of everyone in his class and he might as well have slept in a garbage bag. But he still kept it.

First he lays the tent out on the ground and pins the floor down with L-shaped pegs. Then he slides long metal poles into the two seams at the front and back of the tent. And then he stretches out thin ropes from the two points of the tent and pegs them down into the ground too.

Violet thinks it looks a lot better

than a garbage bag. It looks even better than the bottom-bunk house she made with the sheet at the beach house. Violet thinks it is an excellent tent.

Dylan unzips the front and

starts putting things inside. He puts in his sleeping bag, a pillow, his chess set, his violin, and a flashlight. And then he goes inside and he doesn't come out.

Violet and Mama and Nicola have breakfast. It feels a bit funny without Dylan there, but Mama shows them the part of the newspaper where you can look for a new house and that gives them something to talk about. The people who write the advertisements do it in a special

way to use as few letters as pos-
sible, so instead of "three bedrooms,"
they write "3 bdrms" and instead of
"vegetable garden," they write "veg
grdn." Violet looks to see if there
is one with bnk bds like the beach

house, but she doesn't spot any.

"Are there any you like the look of?" asks Mama.

It is very hard for Violet to imagine living anywhere else, and whenever she tries to think of it, she gets a funny feeling in her throat. She wonders if it's the same sort of feeling Dylan is having.

While Mama is in the shower and Nicola is getting dressed, Violet makes some toast and puts it on a tray with a note that says:

She draws a violin and a violet

again, and then she goes outside and

puts the tray just outside the zip-up

door of Dylan's tent.

"There's some breakfast outside your front door!" she shouts, since you can't knock on a tent.

There isn't any answer, just the slight rustling of a sleeping bag.

But when Violet goes up to her room and looks out the window, the tray has disappeared into the tent.

5 The House Hunt

Over the next few days, Mama and Vincent visit houses they read about in the newspaper. They visit a different one almost every morning because they need to find a house so soon. Sometimes Nicola and Violet go too. Dylan mostly stays in his tent. So far all the houses are either a bit too small, a bit too expensive, or a bit too far away.

Mama says things like, "But where would the dining table fit?" and Vincent says things like, "It might get a bit hot in the summer."

Violet doesn't mind so much about dining tables or hotness in the summer, but she does think that none of the houses look much like a proper home, where people could have dinner and do knitting

and sort through boxes of small things. The new houses smell like paint and soap, not ginger cake or pumpkin soup. There isn't a web in any of the kitchen windows where a small friendly spider could live if it wanted to. And there isn't any music or chatting coming from any of the rooms. There is just the funny empty sound of no furniture.

But as well as house hunting, there is lots of work to do to prepare for the small garden wedding, and Violet likes that much more.

Today Vincent is building a special archway out of wire and bendy branches, big enough for him and Mama to walk under. It will be decorated with leaves and flowers for the wedding, and Violet thinks it will look beautiful in their garden, although it might have to go a bit to the side if Dylan is still living in his tent.

Mama is making a list of people
to invite and then crossing most of
them off again, since it will be quite
a small wedding.

Nicola is folding paper cranes and hanging them on silver strings. They will be gifts for the wedding guests to take home. Violet watches her sister's fingers folding and tweaking and twiddling the little flat white papers until they turn into perfect, pointy birds. It is almost like magic, Violet thinks. She hopes there will be enough for her to have one too.

Violet is drawing pictures of lovely wedding dresses for Mama. Mama will be making the dress with her sewing machine, so she needs lots of good ideas to help with the design. Violet draws long dresses and short dresses, dresses with long trains, matching hats, veils, jewels, flowers, and even one with fairy wings and a wand, which Mama says is actually her favorite,

but maybe not for a wedding. In all the pictures, Violet draws sparkles in Mama's hair.

At lunchtime Violet takes a sandwich, some juice, and a banana

into the garden on a tray for Dylan.
She wonders if they will have to hire
a truck to move Dylan's tent with
him still in it when they finally do
find a new house.

6 The Terrible Storm

Later in the afternoon there is a deep rumbling in the sky.

"I heard on the radio that there was going to be a storm," says Vincent, who has finished working on the wedding archway and come in for a cup of tea.

"What about Dylan?" asks Violet.

"Maybe he'll come inside," says Mama hopefully.

Gray clouds are filling the sky, and it is getting dark even though it's much too early for the sun to be going down. Violet goes outside.

"Dylan," she says. Then she waits. There is a little bit of rustling from inside the tent. "There's going

to be a big storm tonight. Maybe you could come inside, just until it's over."

"No," says Dylan.

"What if your tent leaks?" asks Violet.

"I don't care," says Dylan.

"What if you have to sleep in a puddle?" asks Violet.

"I don't care," says Dylan again.

There is already quite a strong wind blowing, and Mama calls Violet back inside.

Normally, it is nice to be inside the house with your family when there is a big noisy storm outside and there is pumpkin soup for dinner and something on the TV about penguins. But it is hard to enjoy it when your brother is outside in the garden in a leaky tent. Every now and then the sky lights up outside and a big crack of thunder makes everything rattle. All of Violet's insides rattle too.

In every ad break, Violet and

Mama look out the window. Dylan's tent looks more and more like one of Nicola's paper cranes that didn't

quite work out and got crumpled and put in the garbage.

At the end of the penguin program there is the clicking sound of the back door opening. Dylan stands in the doorway, shivering like one of the penguins in the documentary.

Violet has never seen anyone so wet, not even at the beach. There is water dripping from Dylan's nose and his ears. His pajamas, which are completely stuck to him, make little rivers that run into a puddle all round his feet. He is the bluish color of a very cold person.

Mama runs over and hugs him. She doesn't even notice all the

wetness and coldness getting on her. Water drips from the ends of Dylan's frowning eyebrows, and he does not hug her back. He stomps up the stairs, leaving a trail on the carpet behind him like a snail. Then the shower turns on. And a bit later the door of Dylan's room clicks shut. Everyone sighs.

But Vincent gets up.

7 The Purple Package

Vincent rummages in his backpack and gets something out. Before he met Mama, Vincent was a backpacker who traveled all over the world. He says his backpack was like his house, because it had everything he needed in it. He says that when you have to carry everything on your back all the time, you realize you don't actually need very much to survive,

or even to be comfortable and happy.
Even though he is not a backpacker
anymore, he says he will always keep
his backpack, just to remind himself
of that. It is one of the things he has
been storing at Violet's house while
they search for a new one.

Violet wonders if there is a tent
in the backpack that Vincent is going
to give Dylan to replace Dad's old
leaky one. But even though tents can
fold up to be quite small, the thing
Vincent is getting out is much too

small to be a tent. It is a dirty, flattish, purple cloth bag. Violet wonders what could be inside it. She knows it must be something important if it is one of the things Vincent carried on his back all over the world.

Vincent takes the bag upstairs, and there is a little bit of knocking and a lot of quiet talking and then the sound of Dylan's door clicking open. Mama and Violet and Nicola try to pretend they're not listening, but really they all are. They can't make out any words, but they can tell that there is no crossness in the talking.

In the morning the storm is finished and there are voices in the garden.

Violet wakes up and looks out of her window. Vincent is down there with Dylan, and they are dragging everything out of the tent and putting it out in the sun to dry. Dylan's sleeping bag is hanging from the branches of a tree. His pillow and his pillowcase are laid out on the grass, and his violin case (which is waterproof, luckily) and bits and pieces of his chess set are strewn along the path.

While everything is drying in the sun, Dylan and Vincent sit beside the

tent, and Vincent opens the purple cloth bag. Violet watches closely through her bedroom window. Inside the bag is some red, stiffish material; some needles; some green thread; a pair of scissors; and something that looks a bit like a tube of toothpaste, only smaller. Vincent cuts two pieces of material about the same size, and Dylan squeezes stuff from the tube onto them. They put a piece on each side of a hole in the tent and press hard. Then they cut more pieces and stick them over the other holes. Later on, when the stuff from the tube has had time to dry, they sew all around the patches with the needles and green thread, and put more of the stuff in the tube on top of that.

By the time Violet has finished her breakfast, Dylan's tent is covered in red patches with green stitching. And by the time the patching is finished and the tent is back up again, most of Dylan's wet things are almost dry. Violet thinks the tent looks even better with the patches and stitching.

After that, Dylan decides to stay in his tent. Mama, Nicola, Vincent, and Violet wish that he wanted to come back inside the house, but they are glad that at least the tent is not leaky anymore.

All through the day, Violet admires the patchy tent. Later on, in the nighttime, when Violet wakes up, wishing they could all stay forever in their house with the nice smell of ginger cake and the small kitchen spider, she tiptoes over to the window and looks at the tent in the garden. Dylan is awake too and is reading with his flashlight, making the patches glow like stained glass.

8. The Wedding Preparations

It is the day before the wedding, and the Mackerels and Vincent are nearly ready.

They have found a new house with enough rooms for everyone and also room in the back garden for Dylan's tent if he would like to put it up again. Mama says there is enough space for the dining table, and Vincent says it should stay coolish in the summer as long as everyone remembers to pull down the blinds. So now no one has to house hunt anymore, which Violet is glad about. But it does mean that they are really, definitely moving houses, which is a thought that gives Violet's heart a slight squeezing feeling. But everyone except Dylan is busy organizing the last of the special things for the wedding, so there is not much extra time for worrying.

Vincent is finishing the wedding

arch, and all there is left to do is to wind ivy around it and put white flowers on, which they will do in the morning just before the guests arrive, so that it will look nice and fresh. Violet thinks it would look even nicer if it did not have to go next to Dylan's tent. Mama says no one is going to make Dylan move it if he doesn't want to. Violet wonders if he would mind her decorating it with ivy and white flowers so it could at least match the arch.

Mama is adding the finishing touches to her wedding dress. It is long and has a train and tiny pearls sewn on the front called seed pearls, which were from *her* mama's wedding dress.

Violet and Nicola are making sparkles for Mama's hair by gluing some of Nicola's sparkles onto hairpins. And they save some sparkles to glue onto Mama's white slippers so they will match too. When Mama tries it

all on, Violet thinks she looks like a
lady in a magazine. She and Nicola
both stare and stare.

Mama looks at herself in the mirror and twirls. Violet has never seen Mama twirl before, or even look in the mirror much, except when she has been hugging someone who was eating toast and she is checking to see if there is jelly on her. But this is a different sort of looking and twirling. Mama looks like a princess.

At first Violet was a bit disappointed that Mama wasn't going to have wings on her wedding dress, but then Mama had the good idea

that *Violet's* dress could have wings
if she liked. So they have sewn some
onto one of Mama's nightgowns and
trimmed it to the right length and

that is what Violet is going to wear for the wedding.

Nicola is going to wear a party dress that got too short (after she got quite tall). Mama has helped her make some matching pants that go under it.

Vincent is going to wear a waistcoat that Mama made for him. He says he might comb his hair, but he is not making any promises. Violet has never seen Vincent with combed hair before, because when you are a backpacker, you don't bother much with combing. Mama says she doesn't really mind as long as there aren't any actual leaves or twigs in his hair, which there sometimes are when he has been out in the garden working on the wedding arch.

In the evening, when everything is as ready as it can be, Mama writes a letter to Dylan. She puts it in an envelope with a photo. Mama does not show Violet the letter because it is just for Dylan, but she does show her the photo. It is of Mama, Dad, Nicola, and Dylan camping in the tent when it was new, before it got leaky and musty. Mama is holding Nicola's hand, and Nicola is smaller than Violet is now. Even though Dylan is quite a small toddler, he is the tallest in the photo because he is sitting up on Dad's shoulders, smiling and waving.

"Where was I?" asks Violet.

"You hadn't been born yet," says Mama.

It is funny seeing photos of your family before you were born, Violet thinks, but it is a nice photo, especially of Dylan.

Later on, when she is supposed to be in bed, Violet looks out into the garden from her window and sees Mama unzipping the door of Dylan's tent, just enough to post the letter inside.

9

The Early Morning

Violet wakes up very, very early on the morning of the wedding. She thinks about her dress with wings, which is an exciting thought. She also thinks about the new house, which is a worrying thought. Neither thought is very helpful for

getting back to sleep. Violet gets up and looks out her window.

Dylan is sitting in the garden by his tent, looking up at the little bit of morning light starting to creep into the sky. Mama says that when people are in their personal space with the door shut, it means they want to be by themselves. But Dylan is outside, not inside. Violet puts on her dressing gown and slippers and tiptoes downstairs.

"I woke up and I can't get back

to sleep," says Violet, sitting down beside her brother, just in case he is in the mood for talking back.

"Me neither," says Dylan.

He doesn't seem to mind Violet being there.

"How do you go to the bathroom when you live in a tent?" asks Violet.

She has been wondering that for quite a long time.

"You dig a hole if you're doing real camping," says Dylan, "but usually I just sneak inside when you're all busy or out house hunting."

Then they don't say anything for a little while, just think and watch the creeping light. Even though they are not saying anything, Violet wonders if they might be having the same sorts of thoughts. She is thinking mostly about all the different things they have done in the garden together, like the time Dylan made her a teepee out of sticks, and the time he grew mushrooms in a special box and Violet helped him pick them when they were big enough to have with dinner. Violet wonders if, like her, Dylan is wishing and wishing that it could be their garden forever.

"Dylan," says Violet. "Do you have any small things that are a bit special but that you don't really need?"

"Is this for one of your theories?" he asks.

"Sort of," says Violet.

Dylan rolls his eyes, but then he goes inside the tent and rummages. He comes out with an extra pawn from his chess set and a spare key from his violin case.

"Are these okay?"

Violet nods. She puts the cream-colored chess piece and the tiny silver key in her dressing-gown pocket and takes them over to the fennel plant

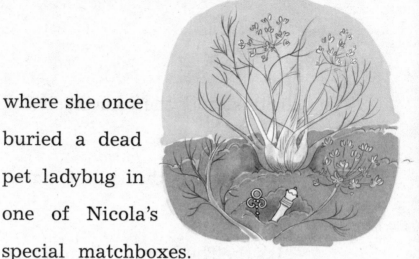

where she once buried a dead pet ladybug in one of Nicola's special matchboxes. There is a small part of Violet there, and a small part of Nicola, and Violet would like there to be a small part of Dylan, too. Dylan watches.

Violet scoops some earth away with her fingers. Then she buries the chess piece and the key and pats the earth smooth on top. The fennel patch looks just the same as it did before, but it is not.

"What's your theory this time?" asks Dylan.

"It's the Theory of Leaving Small Things Behind," says Violet. "When you leave something small behind, maybe a small part of you gets to stay too."

Dylan rolls his eyes again. But then he smiles—just a small smile— for the first time since they were at the beach house.

Violet and Dylan sit for a bit longer. The light has crept over most of the sky now and there are only a few stars left.

"I don't want to leave this house," says Violet. "Even if my theory is right and part of us does get to stay here."

"Me neither," says Dylan.

"But I do want to be where everyone else is, even if it's not this house."

"Me too," says Dylan.

After a while Dylan gets up and starts pulling up the tent pegs.

"What are you doing?" asks Violet.

"I think the garden might look nicer for the wedding without the tent," he says.

Violet helps Dylan to pack everything up, and they carry it all upstairs to his room as quietly as they can. Then they go back outside and Dylan rakes up some leaves and Violet sweeps the path, and they both

look a bit worriedly at the rectangle
of brownish, yellowish dead grass
that had been underneath the tent.
Dylan has the good idea of cover-
ing it with the picnic blanket.
It doesn't look too bad,
Violet thinks, because
it has flowers on
it and is quite
gardenlike.

"What are you two doing?" asks Nicola, coming out in her dressing gown.

"Getting the garden ready," says Violet.

Nicola has a good idea too. She goes back up to her room and brings down some of her extra paper cranes. She threads them on long silver strings and Dylan hangs them from a tree in the garden.

Violet sprinkles some glitter on the path for Mama and Vincent to walk down.

A bit later on Mama comes outside, yawning, with a cup of tea in her hand. "What are you all— Oh!" gasps Mama.

Mama looks around at the freshly raked garden and sees the paper cranes dangling on silver threads, the flowery picnic blanket where the tent was, and the glittery path sparkling in the morning sun.

When Dylan walks over to her and gives her a hug, it almost looks as though Mama is sparkling too.

"Thank you," says Mama, hugging back and smiling and nearly crying a little bit.

10 The Beautiful Wedding

There are quite a few other things to do before the wedding begins. They all help Mama bring out the dining table to put the food and drinks on. Dylan and Violet bring out every chair in the whole house, so that all the guests will have somewhere to sit. Nicola ties white ribbons around each of the chairs so that they will sort of match. When Vincent arrives,

they put up the archway and decorate
it with leaves and flowers.

Then everyone has to get dressed in their wedding clothes. Violet puts on her new dress with wings, and Nicola puts on her dress with matching pants. Vincent puts on his waistcoat and combs his hair, and Dylan puts on the tie that Mama bought him to wear last year when he won a certificate for violin-playing. Mama puts on her beautiful dress. Nicola puts Mama's hair sparkles in, and Violet sprays perfume on Mama. It is all very exciting.

When the guests begin to arrive, Mama and Vincent stay upstairs so it will be a surprise when they all see Mama in her wedding dress and Vincent with his combed hair. Violet, Nicola, and Dylan have to open the door and show everyone where the garden is and which chair is whose.

Nicola's guest is her best friend, Lara. Violet's guest is the old lady Iris MacDonald. They met when Violet was in the hospital having her tonsils out. Iris MacDonald has a beautiful flower garden, and she has made Mama a bouquet with lilies and forget-me-nots. Mama has said it's not too late for Dylan to invite a guest too, so he has asked Tim from next door.

Mama's sister arrives wearing a big hat with flowers and carrying a huge platter of fruit and bread and special cheeses.

Then Vincent's best friend, Buzz, arrives with a cooler full of drinks and ice. Violet has never seen a person

with curlier hair or bigger feet than
Buzz. And if you say, "Hello, Buzz
the Fuzz," he says, "Hello, Violet the
Pilot,"and pretends to be an airplane
and lets you fly him. Violet quite likes
Buzz.

Then the celebrant arrives and it is time for the wedding to begin. All the guests go quiet, and Violet feels a bit nervous. The old lady Iris MacDonald has brought Violet and Nicola each a basket of petals to throw. Everyone is waiting.

Finally Mama and Vincent come out of the back door and everyone claps and Violet and Nicola throw the petals. Mama and Vincent walk along the sparkly path and under the special archway holding hands,

and someone whispers, "Don't they look lovely?"

Violet listens to the celebrant doing lots of talking and Mama and Vincent saying "we will" and "I do." Sometimes the celebrant has to say things twice because her voice is softish and Vincent is a little bit deaf. Then Buzz gives Vincent the ring to put on Mama's finger.

"I now pronounce you husband and wife," says the celebrant.

Dylan quickly gets up from his

chair and goes inside. Mama and Vincent look worriedly at each other. Violet and Nicola look worriedly at each other too.

"Shall I go on?" asks the celebrant.

"Yes, please," says Mama.

"Well, then," says the celebrant, "you may now kiss."

Just then there is a loud bumping noise and everyone, including Mama and Vincent, turns around and looks up. Dylan is in Violet's room, opening the upstairs window as wide as he can. Violet wonders even more worriedly what he is doing.

But then suddenly the garden fills with a lovely sound. It is a tune called "Pachelbel's Canon," and Dylan is playing it on his violin. Mama and Vincent look up with the biggest smiles of all.

"You may *now* kiss," says the celebrant, laughing.

Mama and Vincent kiss while the music plays and everyone claps

and Violet and Nicola throw the rest of their petals.

All afternoon, while everyone is chatting and eating and looking at their paper cranes and Violet the Pilot is flying Buzz the Fuzz like a plane, people keep saying it was a beautiful wedding.

Violet is quite sleepy from her early start, but she thinks it was a beautiful wedding too.

11
The New House

On her very last day in the house Violet has lived in her whole life, it hardly feels like her house at all. Vincent and Buzz have been moving furniture in Buzz's truck, driving it to the new house. Nearly all of the smaller things have been packed up in big cardboard boxes to go in the truck too. The pictures have been taken off the walls and the rugs have been rolled up. Mama is even painting over the special place in the doorway where she used to measure everyone on their birthday and draw a line and write their name and their new age next to it so they could see how much they had grown since last year. She says the new people in the house will probably prefer a doorway without writing and lines.

Mama asks Violet if she would like to help to paint the doorway. Violet definitely would not. What she would like to do is sit on her bed and have a little cry, but her bed is in the truck. So she goes upstairs to where her bed used to be, in the room that will be her personal space for a few more hours. There is one box there. Inside are some of Violet's books and puzzles, a doll, some pencils, and Violet's Box of Small Things, which is mostly full of beads, buttons, and bits of ribbon that she has found and kept. Everything else has been taken down into the truck already.

Violet sits next to the box. She does not close the door because she would actually quite like someone to come in and sit with her, even though they would have to sit on the floor. But everyone is busy.

Violet can hear Mama and Nicola downstairs, talking about the new house. Nicola is quite excited because her new bedroom is going to be bigger than her old one and she has been wanting a bigger room for a long time. Mama is quite excited too because there is going to be a room for her knitting and her sewing things, which have been in baskets and boxes and all over the dining table for too long, she says. Vincent is very excited because he is planning a vegetable patch in the new garden and he has already bought some seedlings and a book about compost.

Dylan has been packing the very last box of things in his room. He is just walking past Violet's room to take it downstairs when he sees her.

"Are you all right in there, Violet?" he asks.

"Yes," says Violet. But a big tear is trickling down the side of her nose. Dylan puts his box down and comes in and gives her a hug. There was no furniture in his tent either, so he doesn't mind sitting on the floor.

"Our house is all empty and echoey," says Violet. "It doesn't even look like our house anymore. It feels as if none of us have ever lived here."

"I know what you mean," says Dylan. All the tissues are packed away in boxes, but he wipes Violet's big tear away with his sleeve. He doesn't say anything, but Violet thinks that just knowing someone else feels a bit the same as you do can be just as helpful sometimes.

After a while, Dylan says, "Want to see something?" Violet does, so Dylan takes her into his room.

He shows Violet a little space where the windowsill doesn't quite meet the wall.

"I was thinking about the Theory of Leaving Small Things Behind," he says. He has tucked a tiddlywink in there, from the tin Dad gave him when he was much younger.

"Now maybe a part of you will get to stay here forever," says Violet.

"That's what I thought," says Dylan.

Just then Vincent calls up the stairs, "Come on, you two, we're loading the last boxes into the truck now."

"I'd better take our boxes down,"

says Dylan. "Will you be all right?"

"Yes," says Violet.

Before Dylan takes the last of Violet's things downstairs, she pulls out her Box of Small Things.

"I'll need this just for a minute," she says.

When Dylan has gone downstairs with the others and she is all by herself again, she pulls up the carpet in the corner of her room where it has always curled up a little bit. Underneath the carpet are wooden floorboards with thin little cracks between them. Violet pushes a small red button into one of the cracks and then smooths the carpet back down again. It looks exactly as it did a moment before.

Next Violet goes over to the other corner of the bedroom where the thick paint on the walls has peeled a little bit. Standing on her tiptoes, she tweaks a tiny gold sequin in behind the peel of paint. Nobody would ever guess it was there.

Finally she goes over to the window and feels behind the curtains for the string you pull to make them open and close. She ties a small piece of purple ribbon around the string and pushes it up as high as she can. It will probably never be noticed by anyone.

When she has finished, she closes her Box of Small Things and gets ready to leave her room for the very last time. Everyone is calling her from downstairs and saying, "Hurry up, Violet!" and "Get a move on, please!" but she turns around for just one last look at her empty room.

Places, even personal spaces, look the same after Violet has been in them. But they are not.